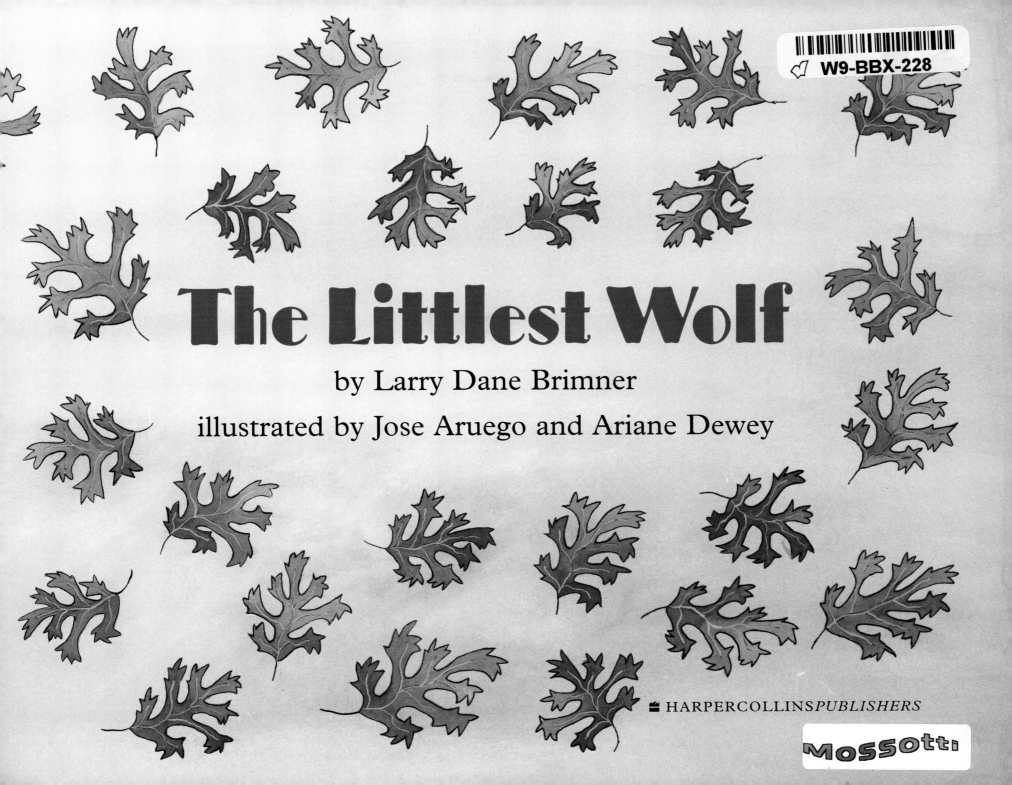

The Littlest Wolf

by Larry Dane Brimner

illustrated by Jose Aruego and Ariane Dewey

HARPERCOLLINSPUBLISHERS

It was a perfect summer morning. Big Gray was watching his pups
frolic in a poppy-dappled meadow. But not all of them frolicked.

One pup, the littlest, peeked out at the others
from behind the trunk of a great, gnarled oak.

Big Gray ambled up beside the little wolf. He scratched softly behind his furry ears. "Little One, why aren't you playing with your sister and brothers?" he asked.

The little wolf began to fidget with an acorn that rested on the ground beside his paw. "Frankie said that I do not roll in a straight line," he said.

Big Gray thought for a moment. He scratched his chin. "Straight lines can be a bother," he said. "Show me."

It won't do any good, thought the little wolf. But he curled himself into a ball anyway and rolled— feet over head, head over feet. Again and again.

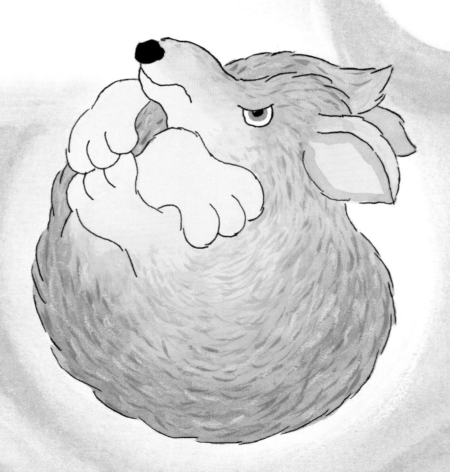

The little wolf zigged.

The little wolf zagged.

The little wolf zigged and zagged.

"See?" he said to Big Gray when at last he stopped rolling. "I do not roll in a straight line."

"No," said Big Gray. "Little One does not roll in a straight line like Frankie. Little One rolls in a line with curves." Big Gray was thoughtful again. "That is just as it should be."

"Are you sure?" the little wolf asked.

"I am sure," said Big Gray. "Lines without curves come later."

"That is good to know," said the little wolf. And he rolled to the middle of the meadow and back again, zigging and zagging all the way.

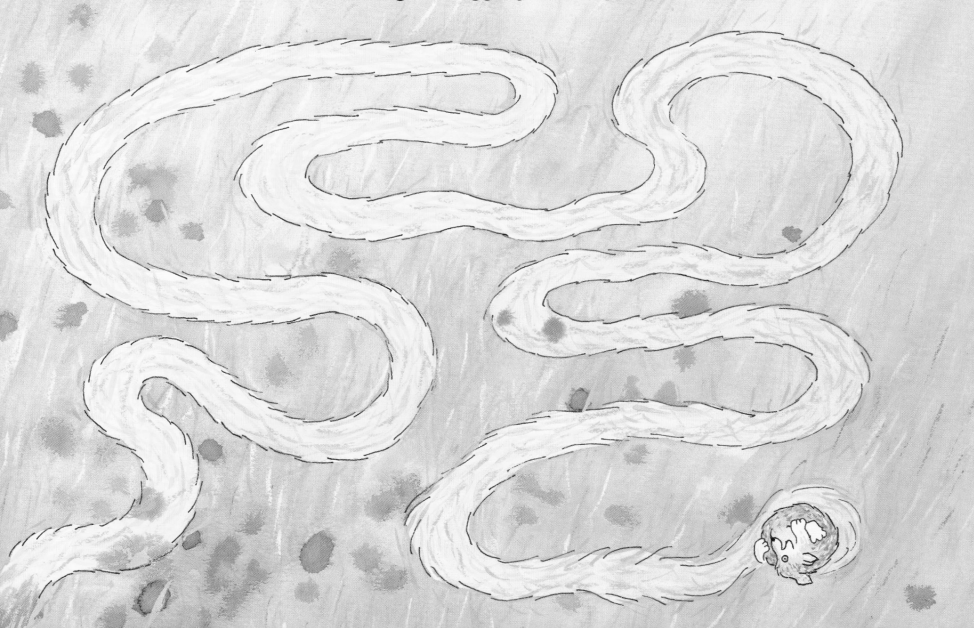

But still something bothered the little wolf. He tugged at Big Gray's fur, and Big Gray bent his head so the pup could whisper in one ear. "Ana says I am a slowpoke," the little wolf said.

Big Gray looked out at the meadow where Ana was bounding after a monarch. "Slowpoke, you say?" He scratched his chin. "Show me," he said.

It won't do any good, thought the little wolf. But he took a deep breath anyway and started to run.

Before the little wolf had gotten very far, his run had become a galumph.

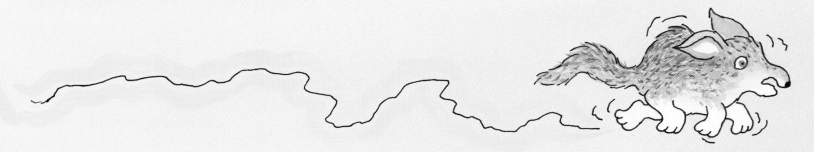

And soon after, it was just a toddle.

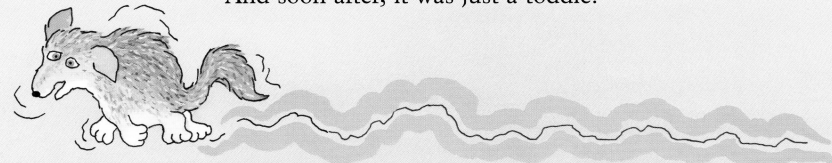

He galumphed and toddled. He toddled and galumphed.

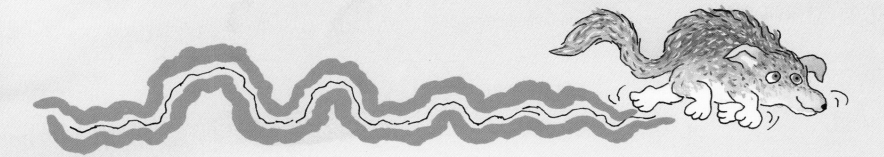

"See?" the little wolf said to Big Gray when at last he came back. "I am a slowpoke."

Big Gray nodded. "It is true that Ana runs like the wind and you run like a soft breeze," he said. "That is just as it should be."

"Are you sure?" the little wolf asked.

"I am sure," said Big Gray. "Running like the wind comes later."

"That is good to know," said the little wolf. And he galumphed to the middle of the meadow and toddled back again.

"Big Gray—," the little wolf started. But before he could finish, the words got stuck. So he pitched an acorn into the waving grass, and then another.

Big Gray rested his huge paw on the little wolf's shoulder. "What is it, Little One?" he asked gently.

The little wolf looked up at Big Gray. "Will—will I ever pounce as high as Tyler?"

"Tyler pounces as high as the oaks," said Big Gray.

"Tyler pounces as high as the *clouds*," said the little wolf.

Big Gray nodded. "Pouncing THAT high can be a bother," he said, scratching his chin. "Show me your pounces."

It won't do any good, thought the little wolf. But he crouched close to the ground anyway and sprang into the air.

He pounced through the tall green grass.

He pounced between waving poppies.

He pounced onto a small pile of granite rocks. And then off again.

"See?" he said to Big Gray when at last he was finished pouncing. "I do not pounce as high as the clouds. I do not even pounce as high as the oaks."

"No," said Big Gray. "It is true that you do not pounce as high as the clouds. But you do not need to. You pounce as high as the poppies, and"—Big Gray nodded—"that is just as it should be."

"Are you sure?" the little wolf asked.

"I am sure," said Big Gray. "High pounces come later."

"That is good to know," said the little wolf. And he pounced through the grass and between the poppies all the way to the middle of the meadow and back again. And not once did he need to pounce as high as the oaks or clouds.

"You are right, Big Gray," said the little wolf when he returned, very pleased with himself. "I pounce high enough."

"You certainly do," said Big Gray.

Then they sat together in the warm summer sun, the big wolf and the little one, until the little wolf started to yawn.

"I think it's time for a nap," Big Gray said, and he called his other pups to join him.

Then Big Gray and his four pups lay together as a gentle breeze softly ruffled their fur. Big Gray looked up at the great gnarled oak above them. "Remember the acorns, Little One," he whispered in the little wolf's ear.

"They are just as they should be.
And look what they become."